Jean Demetris
Illustrated by Alex Demetris

Grandma's Box of Memories

Helping Grandma to Remember

Jessica Kingsley *Publishers*
London and Philadelphia

First published in 2014
by Jessica Kingsley Publishers
73 Collier Street
London N1 9BE, UK
and
400 Market Street, Suite 400
Philadelphia, PA 19106, USA

www.jkp.com

Library of Congress Cataloging in Publication Data
A CIP catalog record for this book is available from the Library of Congress

British Library Cataloguing in Publication Data
A CIP catalogue record for this book is available from the British Library

ISBN 978 1 84905 517 8
eISBN 978 1 78450 013 9

Printed and bound in China

For George

Hello, I'm Alice.

My Grandma and Grandpa were always fun to be with.

Me, my brother and my little sister spent lots of time with them doing lovely things.

Then Grandma began to get confused sometimes.

Now, on some days Grandma is forgetful, and on other days she is *very* forgetful.

Dad explained that Grandma has dementia. People with dementia find it difficult to remember things, such as people's faces, how to use the telephone and even birthdays.

Dad and I talked about what I could do to help Grandma remember things. Soon she may not even recognise us any more, but we will still remember all the good times we shared with her.

I had an idea! I would find a box and fill it with things that gave Grandma and us pleasure.

What can I put in the box?

I know! I will put in some pretty packets of flower seeds.

Grandma and I had lots of happy times planting seeds and watching them grow into beautiful flowers.

I wonder what Grandpa will put in the box...

He wants to put in a photograph of
their wedding day.

It was a very happy day and Grandma looked so beautiful.

What will Mum put in the box?

Mum wants to put in a long, colourful piece of knitting.

Grandma taught Mum how to knit and on winter days they would knit scarves for Mum's teddy bears.

What will Dad put in the box?

Dad wants to put a CD of children's songs in the box.

We used to sing these songs in the car when we took Grandma to the seaside.

What will my brother Harry put in the box?

He wants to put some toy animals in the box.

He says maybe the toys will remind Grandma of our fun visits to the zoo, when the chimpanzees made us laugh.

What will my little sister Ellie put in the box?

She wants to put in a big wooden spoon.

Grandma used to make cakes with us and let us lick the spoon... Yummy!

Aunt Lucy heard about the box and she wanted to put something in...

A bag of lavender.

Grandma always put lavender bags in her wardrobe to make her clothes smell lovely.

Grandma might remember the smell.

Alice, Harry and Ellie gave the box to Grandma.

They all enjoyed looking through it and remembering the fun they had together.

Now, when Grandma gets upset
Grandpa plays the CD to her.

Hearing the songs makes her feel happy again,
and often she remembers the words.

When Grandma feels confused, Mum and Dad look at the piece of knitting with her.

The softness of the wool and remembering the scarves she used to knit for Mum's teddy bears makes Grandma feel calm again.

What a lot of memories in Grandma's box!

What would you put in?

A Note for Adults

Dementia is a progressive condition that causes memory loss and difficulties with reasoning and communication. Daily tasks such as cooking, using equipment such as the telephone and caring for oneself become more challenging.

Coping with the illness can be distressing for everyone involved – children as well as adults.

Children may be aware that something is wrong but confused about what exactly it is. They will be able to deal better with their feelings once the diagnosis is explained to them. It is natural for an adult to want to protect the child yet it is important to explain what is going on in a calm and clear way. Children need reassurance that adults are there for them and can offer them time for discussion, by both talking and listening, and encouraging them to ask questions.

Children may experience a range of feelings, such as sadness, anxiety, anger and confusion. Most of all, children may experience a sense of loss that the person with dementia is not the same as they once were.

It is important that children understand that dementia cannot be cured but that there are ways that they can help the person with dementia to feel loved and wanted.

This book, *Grandma's Box of Memories*, attempts to address some of the issues Alice faces when her Grandma is diagnosed with dementia. It is intended to be used as an educational and entertaining tool to help children to understand and help with the effects of dementia in older people.

Alice talks with her dad and explores ways in which she can help Grandma. She involves all the family members, and asks them to select a favourite item to put in Grandma's box of memories. All of the chosen items have a personal relevance to Grandma and the family member.

These items are carefully chosen to refer to the five senses: sight, taste, touch, smell and hearing. Since sounds are often the easiest memories to recall, music and singing play a very important role in stimulating the memory of people with dementia.

The book ends with an invitation for children to add their own ideas, and thus acts as a prompt for discussion and personal thoughts.

We hope that the book will be useful to both adults and children who are having to deal with a difficult situation and that it brings them some lightness, laughter and love.